I0590948

WARM
RAINY
SENSATIONS
Short Stories by Brian Robinson Sr.

Warm Rainy Sensations

Short Stories by: Brian Robinson Sr.

Cover created and designed by: Jazzy Kitty Publishing

Logo designs by: Andre M. Saunders and Leroy Grayson

Editor: Anelda Attaway/Co-Editor: Brian Robinson Sr.

Jazzy Kitty Publishing

ACKNOWLEDGMENTS

I want to thank God for the gift of writing. I want to also thank all the people, especially the ladies that have encouraged me on this journey. This encouraging support is one of the reasons why I write.

Special thanks to YBH Production, L Bell Promotions, Beesrain Promotions, and Biiwiir Productions for their marketing and support.

Last and not least, thank you to Anelda Attaway and the staff at Jazzy Kitty Publishing.

DEDICATIONS

Ladies, you have inspired me through countless discussions through friendships as well as intimate relationships. Therefore, I dedicate this book to you and all the secret desires you often keep locked away. It's time to release and explore. May you all enjoy each short story, and come away wanting more.

PRELUDE

So she wonders what he's thinking when he kisses her! He holds her so tight, and it's so intense. He never closes his eyes, and he never takes them off her. This guy is deep and she's thinking it's way past the point of him being impressive. She's thinking to herself, *no this passion is real!* So she wonders, how much of me should I leave for him of my own free will? How much should I leave for him to take by his loving force? How much to show him of what I already know? How much of what I really want might scare him off or give him second thoughts about where I've been in my life? Still thinking to herself, *she wonders, why am I so worried about everything and why can't I just go wit the flow? I bet all he's thinking is it's too hard to put it away now! It's none of his goddamn business where I've been, he didn't ask before he got his faucet running, or those two little eyes popping out of my tight T-shirt, damn it!* Oops! Let me slow down; I'm busting my own groove. Ain't no way I'm gonna block my own cock. Still thinking to herself, *I want...no I need to open up this time. I'm feeling really selfish. I don't wanna boost his ego, and I don't wanna worry about bruising it either. I wanna bruise him! I wanna love so hard this time that he's gonna need a hot bath to recover! I don't wanna give myself to him; I wanna take him!*

(How many women have felt like this?)

SHE WONDERS?

TABLE OF CONTENTS

INTRODUCTION

Brian Robinson Sr., shares with us his erotic writings titled Warm Rainy Sensations...Urban Fiction love tales at its best!!! Inside you will find three short stories, and they will keep you wanting more.

Brian introduces to you Where She Wants to Be, SHY, and The Sadie Hawkins Surprise and you won't be disappointed. Especially the ladies.

WHERE SHE WANTS TO BE

WHERE SHE WANTS TO BE

He approaches her...his eyes fixed into the center of her eyes, staring deep into her soul so much that he has no idea she'd smoothly stepped out of her heels the moment that he closed the bedroom door. She stands there a few inches shorter with her belt undone; he places his warm palm on the left side of her sweet caramel colored face. Then he slowly moves his hand around the back of her neck and kisses her cheekbone with his mouth slightly open, while softly and gently sucking her face before barely letting go. As he placed both hands on her face, he kisses her forehead very slightly, and then slides down to her other cheek before kissing her chin. He then takes a mouthful of her bottom lip and sucks it painlessly as she thinks to herself how warm and soft his lips feel. She begins to assert herself, and she grabs the sides of his T-shirt near his waist and pulls him closer so that her breast pushes against the lower part of his chest as she offers her lips to his again and adds the warmth of her tongue. Suddenly, there is a rise of energy through their bodies as she moves him back just enough to pull his T-shirt over his head and to the floor. She decides to have a soft bite of his chest with her lips and tongue, and before she knew it, her jeans were next to his shirt on the floor. She didn't remember taking them off, and she didn't care.

Normally, he wouldn't mind an assertive woman, but this being their first time and him feeling things he's never felt before for a woman, this had to be all about her and him giving his all to her. This was love and love making with a start of a beginning with no purpose of an end, concluding was not even an afterthought. He put his hand on the highest part of her waist and while sucking her bottom lip and gently biting it, he lifts her up. She wraps her legs around his waist as he takes just a few steps to the bed and sits her at the foot of it. He clutches her thighs and lifts her legs to remove the dark-blue lace boy shorts. She glances at him, and wonders where his pants and boxers went so fast. No matter, no worries, this is **where she wants to be**.

She relaxes into the role of following his lead, intrigued by the emotion and passion in each touch and kiss, and in the fact that he hasn't scoped out her body yet now noticing the ten pounds that she took off just for this weekend. He hasn't viewed those sugar, walnut, sister style hips that run wild in her family; yet her eyes still commanding his full attention. He's locked into her soul through those eyes, and she's about to open more than just what's needed for this physical act, and she knows it. He's going to touch more than just the warmest and wettest part of her throbbing body tonight; he's also visiting her heart and soul, and all windows, doors, and walls are open only to him.

She scoots up to the top of the bed as he steps up, now standing over her, he drops to his knees, and is now in-between her feet. He lifts her left leg with his right hand and begins to kiss the arch in her foot. He works his way up to her ankle and up to suck on her calf, and then as he slowly heads down to her inner thigh, she thinks to herself, "What patience after all this time." At an instant, she's reminded of what he said about when this night came; that if possible he would need all day, all afternoon, all evening, overnight, and into the morning, and remembering how he never smirked, smiled, or made light of it in any way even though she did. Now she gets how serious he really was.

He places his right hand on her pelvis while continuing to kiss down her inner thigh, his hand spreads out just enough to massage the places she wants him to touch the most. As he brings his lips closer to his hand and begins to kiss the places she wants him to kiss the most, her stomach tightens as her legs stiffen up. She closes her eyes, and she feels pressure building inside her. He is now touching, massaging, and kissing deeply into her special needs with the most tender care, yet with passionate force, taking care of her body as if it was made only and especially for him. No matter what roads they traveled to get to this point it's where they need to be. She tells herself, "Breathe girl don't pass out."

HIS LUCKY NUMBER 13... She's still bracing for herself not to explode just yet. This is pleasingly unfamiliar to her; it's their first time together, and they have both waited far too long, but in their minds, they've done this a dozen of times. Now passing all that, as she arches her back, he eases the deep kissing to move onto her stomach and onto her breast. He places his left hand underneath the arch in her back and with his thumb and two fingers on her bra clip, and it's smoothly undone. He grabs hold of it with his teeth; she helps him slide it off, and away as he begins to attend to the perkiness that lay underneath the now discarded matching bra picked out for this special occasion. The warmth of his full lips and tongue over her reminds her of a warm and steamy shower as he wets her two tender spots just before he kisses them with gentle suction style kisses. His closely cropped beard and mustache tickled her areola, and she displays a comforting partial smile from that pleasure. He's taking his time and enjoying every second.

To this point, nothing else on his body has touched her as he's been up on his hands and knees straddling her, loving her exclusively with his lips and tongue. Now he wants to press his body into hers. He dips his hips to slide down between her thighs as he kisses and licks her stomach again, working his way back up pass her perkiness and onto her neck. His chest meets with hers, her lips with his and now the most throbbing and pulsating highly excited part of his body is now introduced to that of hers. They instantly bond, fitting together perfectly and warmly transferring her wetness onto him. His neck rises with a twitch; her head turns ever so slightly, meeting at the same time again to share another passionate kiss.

Finally, their bodies are one; moving in and out and from side to side, at the same time with a bit of a circular twist in perfect harmony as if they are listening to the same Luther Vandross song. The pace quickens and they switch gears, together they start to sweat, and their dripping wet bodies begin to melt into one another, slowly becoming one soul, and then he says it, "I'm not gonna stop." "Please don't," she says. As the pace continues to quicken, he puts his elbow just above her shoulders and moves deeper inside her. He lightly grabs a hand full of her hair as she reaches around his hips and aides in the force of his thrust and the pace. It's building inside of her and it's all happening at once, and she can no longer hold it. To avoid the scream that she's been holding for the last hour, she takes a huge soft bite of his chest and sucks as hard as she can, causing the painful pleasure to heighten his thrust. As he increases his pace and shakes his head in pleasure; she digs her fingers into him. They are climbing the same mountain on opposite sides, seconds away from a warm and watery clash at their peaks. His grip tightens, her grip tightens, his arms lock, her arms lock as they experience *the watery clash*. She lets out a groan with a moan; he lets out a love grunt. One of her legs trembles out of her control as both his legs jumps but then stops, their eyes meet again. She smiles, still with his serious face he says to her, "Wow a month ago you asked me was all this worth the wait; well, I waited all my life for the last 12 hours today; I took you as my wife, I flew over some beautiful mountains despite a fear of flying, I made love to my wife and soulmate for the very first time. I think we just made our first child, and just in case we didn't, we got all night to try some more, I can't put worth on that!" He gently rubs his hands across the top of her slender shoulder and around the back of her as she rubs the top of his head, and they cuddle up tight.

Later after exhausting themselves twice more, they fall off to sleep. It's the perfect end to a beautiful time. After a few more hours go by, he is awakened by the nonstop phone ringing. Just as he's thinking who could be calling this late, then comes a stern knock on the door, and someone calling his name.

THE END. Part 1

SHY

SHY

So she didn't know much about him, but he lives in the building across from her. She thinks he's really sexy, not too good looking though a bit rough around the edges. She has a nickname for him because she doesn't know his name, yet she refers to him as "ruggedly handsome" when she tells her sister about him. Her sister jokes with her that they wouldn't make a cute couple, that's because she's really beautiful like all black women are, but even more because she never had a bad day in her life as far as her looks goes. She's been so beautiful for so long, that even if she turned ugly she'd still think she was beautiful. Her sister asks, "Why are you so drawn to him?" "There is something about him that says he's ok with who and what he is, and he's not too girly about himself. And when he sees me, he's not afraid to stare and kind of gives me a nod of approval when he says hello, and he always says hello," she replied. Her sister asks, "What's all that noise?" "I'm looking for my special weapon, the tight white shorts; I'm gonna speed him up a bit," she answered. "Bye hooker I'm hanging up!" she said. "Good cause I need to wash my hair so it can get curly for me. The peach tank top, the tight white shorts, and my new sandals with the hot high heels; if we ain't rap'n tomorrow his ass is gay, and he's gonna be my new "bbf", anyway, bye girl," she replied.

After she hangs up, she sits on her windowsill and peeks at him. He always sits outside after he plays ball and puts on his sunshades even though the sun is on its way down. He pulls out a book and starts writing and every so often, he looks up at the sky. She thinks he's writing a song or something because he appears to be in deep concentration.

Shy gets herself ready for work the next day and ready for bed, knowing she'll be thinking of him all night again. Although she doesn't even know his name or anything about him, she does know a few parts of his routine every other day, like when he plays ball or works out up the street. She's far from home, fresh out of college, and getting settled at her new job. Her brain is running high lately, and she needs rest. Just as she feels the burn just wearing off from finally closing her eyes, the buzzer rings. At first, she thinks she's just imagining it, but then it rings a second time. She looks down from her window, and it's him. There are lots of people still out, so she's not worried. She thinks, "Maybe he knows I watch him!" She's embarrassed quite a bit, but still answers, "Hi who's there?" He answers, "Hi my name is Stacey Carter; I live across the street from you, and I sit outside every other evening. I see you don't miss a night to take in the view, and I wanted to know if you would like to join me outside?" She answers, "I just washed my hair and how did you know which bell to ring?" He replies, "The guy at the desk told me!" "Oh really?" she said. "We use to work together," he stated, "so are you coming down or are we going to converse this way?" "My hair is wet man," she replies and thinking to herself, *I look crazy right now!* "I could come up," he indicated. Shy thinks to herself I wish you would! But instead she says, "I don't know you like that man; you look kinda crazy too!" Stacey laughs and suggests either she come down or he could call a police officer to introduce the two in person. She laughs and says, "The police would crack you in your head if you call them for that." He replied, "My dad use to be the Chief of Police, so they would let me slide with the getting cracked in the head thing. But he wouldn't like it though! By the way, what's your name because I only know you as 4-B and the guy at the desk wouldn't tell me your name?" "My name is Shyler Wells, but you can call me Shy," she said. "So are you coming down Shy?" he asked again. "No, but give me three minutes, and then you can come up to the 4th floor lobby; we can talk there. Listen for the buzzer and behave yourself, or I'll mace your ass," said Shy. They both laugh, but she's shaking up her can of mace at the same time.

Stacey goes up and gets off the elevator, but it doesn't look like he just got finished playing ball. He smells really good to her, and as they shake hands she's thinking to herself, *goddamn he looks better up close*. He's making me wanna get dressed and go out for a drink, or undressed and stay in with drinks. But I'm in training; a new job and fresh out of college! Stay focused girl; I don't wanna get caught up, but I do want some. I've been sitting on my windowsill lusting over this dude for weeks now, and he just pops up at my door. Did I make this happen by watching him? I wonder if he's here just because he knows I've been watching him. Am I just lonely or does he have the sexiest lips I have ever seen? Ok, he's not getting any, but he ain't leaving here without me sucking one of those big lips!"

Shy decides to really talk to him; no cat and mouse just Q&As and asking him to do his best to try to be open and honest. When he talks to her, she advises him that it will only benefit him to talk openly because in her mind, if he fits the build, then he might be built to fit. This is not what she's use to, but she is single and busy and mostly all business for the last six years of schooling and kitty needs to play.

Shy and Stacey have been talking for nearly five hours. They are both wide open with one another, and she starts to wonder if this strong, sexy, and confident man even knows that he's the prey and not the hunter, and that he just happened to stumble into her nest. She's trying to figure out if she's gonna go hard, or take it easy on him, and if it's gonna be tonight because she can make that choice. She's in control of her own desires! This is a first for Shy, and she's not use to having these kinds of desires for a man whom she knows so little about or use to feeling this lonely. Back home she always got plenty of attention by being so perfectly beautiful.

The time is getting more and more right for something unusual to happen, and not only does Shy now desire him, she happens to like him too! They are now really feeling each other! Sitting in the lobby chairs face to face, hearts are racing, and both sets of eyes batting back and forth, Stacey whispers, "I think I could do this all night." Shy slightly hits him and asks, "What else can you do all night?" She catches him completely off guard; although his blood rushes to the proper place, he gives the correct but part one of his answer. He slides his chair a bit closer and puts his cheek against hers, wets his lips, and lets them touch her ears while he whispers back, "Kiss you all over Shy." She slides back a bit, makes eye contact and says, "I thought you would say make love to me." "That's what anyone who just wants you would say, the truth is, we are not in love, and we've barely met, but sometimes we want what we want and I really want you. So if you let me, I'll take my time and treat you the best I can, you will not be disappointed," he replied. Shy takes a deep sigh, grabs his hands, and rises to her feet. She stands in front of him, putting her right hip against his face, rubs her hands on his head while pressing his face against her pelvic area. He looks up at her and she says, "Come be close to me."

Within seconds, he rises to both feet as she grasps his hand, then walks him down the hall and unlocks her door, leading him into her heaven.

Just inside the apartment doors Shy notices that his hands are a little extra warm, but she likes it! She tells him she wants to freshen up a bit and asks him if he would like to use the bathroom to do the same, but Stacey tells her that he's ok. She goes into the bathroom and runs the shower, as he gets comfortable on the couch. Within minutes, the bathroom door opens with a cloud of steam rushing out and Shy reappears with a towel barely covering her frame. She walks up to him and pulls him to follow her into the steamy bathroom. She drops her towel just before the door closes. She pulls his shirt over his head as he's dropping his shorts. At the same time, she's looking down and liking what she has found, that all his systems are a go. She steps into the shower while leading him into the hot steamy water where he receives his first of tonight's showers. The water hits his face, and she places the first kiss with a mixture of warm water sliding into both of their mouths. Stacey's willing to hold off and let her explore since she seems very comfortable leading him to this point, and he likes where she's heading, but he won't resist his natural urge to kiss her beautiful face, lips, and neck in that order, but much slower. He works his way down between her firm petite breasts while rolling his hands over her silky wet body before he drops down to one knee to rub his tongue on her navel. Shy lets out an arousing moan over the sound of the splashing water as he licks and kisses her pelvic area, then slowly turns her around and tongue kisses the small of her back with both his hands and firmly grips her smooth rear end before gently spreading it apart.

Stacey is an educated man in the art of making love. She can sense it just by his touch. Shy decides to let him work on her a bit as she passes him her loofah and her peach scented body wash. She then places her hands on the wall of the shower keeping her legs apart for him to wash and explore her body. She thinks to herself, "Let him freely touch and he will freely taste." Shy is more than just in the mood for something special, and he's starting off real good with the kissing and the touching, its perfect rub, more touching and more kissing, she's in wet watery ecstasy and her first rain is arriving as he is still on her outer body. Her stomach clutches with excitement and she whispers to herself, "WTF!" Her legs are shaking, her body is weak and defenseless and nothing is meaning more to her than this moment. It's a first for her and she's wondering where all that rain came from and why so premature. She has just experienced her first orgasm of the night, although he physically applied his lips and tongue to her body, he has just grazed her surface.

Stacey rises up, still working his tongue while running it up the small of her back, sucking select spots until he reaches her neck. As his tongue reaches the back of her left ear, he whispers to her, "Can I have more please?" Shy replies, "Do whatever you want baby!" He turns her around, puts his right arm under her left thigh and lifts her up while pressing her back against the shower wall. She reaches and grabs the showerhead to brace herself as he lowers her down onto him for a watery entry. Now everything Shy has been holding back is all beginning to surface. She wanted to wait a little longer until they reached her bed, but it's already on. Shy grabs the top of the shower door and pulls herself up to push herself down onto him again, but in a real nice rhythm. The groove is tight again, and she whispers, "WTF!" After just thirteen more minutes of smooth, warm, watery exercise that seemed like thirty seconds to Shy, "WTF" IT'S HAPPENING AGAIN!!! She lets out a little loud this time; she can't stop her arms from shaking; she can't stop her legs either; she's flinging her head back and forth, and lets out another passionate moan. She opens her mouth and takes a mouth full of water and releases it onto his head before releases herself once again. "_-_" They both lean against the warm brick tile of the shower wall, Shy's arms still wrapped around Stacey's neck as he lowers himself down until they meet eye to eye again. She can't believe how opened she allowed herself to be so soon, though she's been craving him from afar. Just for a second she's a bit embarrassed until she realizes that he still hasn't gotten his yet, and she is excited about the work she still has to do.

Shy says to Stacey, "Don't dry off, just come out in two minutes." She jumps out the shower and runs out the bathroom door. Stacey puts his head back under the water for the two minutes as she instructed. After the two minutes are up, he steps out of the shower, water still dripping from his strong sturdy shoulders that sit atop of his not perfect, but pleasing to the female eye real man size body. He takes a deep breath in his nakedness and opens the door.

The room just outside the bathroom is lit up with candles leading down the hall into the bedroom. Gerald Levert is playing in the background. Stacey steps out of the bathroom, walks down the hall, and approaches the bedroom door. As he pushes it open very slowly, Shy's beautiful body is laying across the bottom of the bed. "I'll dry you off if you like?" she said. He replies, "Let's keep things wet ok!" She displays a devilish grin as he approaches. His bloods rushes up again as he grabs her left ankle and puts her toe in his mouth while massaging her tender calf. He opens her legs and slides his tongue down her inner thigh as he kisses all the way through to her pelvic bone, kissing more deeply before working his way to her naval. Shy places her hand on his head and whispers to him, "Can we do it real slow?" "Like it's never gonna end," he replies, and then adds another deep kiss, this time between her petite breasts. She arches her back to prepare for his entry once again as he rises up on her, anticipating that warm, thick, and perfect fitting feeling from him. Her bottom lip quivers as things begin to moisten once again. He reaches around her neck, grabs a hand full of her short wet hair, and forces her face against his chest where she decides to take a light tender bite. So much passion and rhythm amongst them as their hips slowly grind together, and then up and apart as they share glances of admiration for the perfect feeling they're creating between the two. Stacey receives light pricking scratches on his back as he comes down and grinds deep into her. They experience such pleasure on and on and on for nearly forty minutes before they begin to meet at that watery finish that their bodies are sooooo craving at this point. Shy feels her stomach welling up. Stacey's arms and legs begin to shake. Their beautiful and handsome faces begin to twist. She loses control of her legs, and his head uncontrollably trembles. As he looks up at the head of the bed, he notices two of the seven shaking candles just blow out. Shy screams out again, "WTF!" He grumbles. "FUCK MEEEE!!!!!!" To Shy, everything goes dark and her breathing is heavy and deep.

Everything is dark because she has the cover over her head. "He really worked me into a deep sleep," that's her first thought! Shy pulls the cover back and it appears to be morning already. She checks the clock and it reads 7:15. She can't tell if it's morning or evening, but her bed is soaking wet. Shy jumps up and runs to the bathroom and there is water on the floor, but no sign of her sexy love. "Where is Stacey?" she asks herself. "Well I guess he had to get home," she says. She walks over to the window and there he sits out on his normal spot glancing up and looking back down, but the street is busy like it's evening again. "How could that be, I know I didn't sleep through the whole damn day and miss my job, no freaking way," she said. Shy is scared and confused. She grabs her shoes and robe and runs out the door to the elevator, hops on and hits the button three times when finally the door closes. She bolts out at the ground floor walking at a fast pace to the door and across the street. As she's walking up to Stacey, he turns his head suddenly when someone calls him from his building. "Stacey, Staaaacey, hey, you're gonna miss it babe, come on hurry!" she yelled. Shy looks over and can barely see the woman in the doorway holding open the door. Stacey never even looks at her. He gets up and gives a smile to the young lady, and runs off to the doors where she reaches for his hand and they run inside together, leaving his writing pad there on the stoop in his favorite spot. Shy is still confused as she's trying to approach the spot that he just abandoned, thinking to herself, *I might get my razor and peel his whole face when he comes back out here.* But then she reaches his stoop and glances down at his pad. She freezes as if she just saw a ghost. There is a beautiful drawing of her in such amazing detail that it was like her looking into a mirror. Shy wants to run, but she can't move her legs. "WTH is going on?" she's wondering. She turns and asks a man parking his car, "What's today's date?" "Thursday the 12th," he replies. Shy stands very still, it seemed like five minutes had past. "Are you sure?" she asks the man. "Yes! Tomorrow is Friday the 13th, I took off from work. I always take off on Friday the 13th cause I got fired once on that day so it's bad luck for me," he replied. Shy whispers, "WTF". Shy walks away from Stacey's stoop very fast while talking to herself, "It can't still be Thursday, how can that be? Shit was so wet, so real my legs hurt. No, no I got a fucking headache. I need to lie down." She runs into her building and back to her apartment, sits on the edge of her bed, lays back, and falls into a deep sleep again, but is soon awakened by her alarm clock to morning music. Shy jumps up and walks over to her window to find the morning streets bare, and as usual, turns to the mirror and says, "Well we'll always have Thursday." And scoots down the hall to the bathroom and into that memory filled shower.

Shy has begun to surface back to reality but the memory of "ruggedly handsome" still has her floating under Thursdays spell. In and out, she comes and goes as she gets prepared for her workday with the new law firm. Today is a big day for the firm and for Shy, and she needs to clear her head and focus. She has already decided to put some heavy curtains up this evening, which is a good start.

She gets to the office building and pulls into the parking lot where she exits her car. All eyes are definitely on her. She's extra early and as usual dress to the "T" in her own special style that she likes to call "BPSB", BUSINESS PROFESSIONAL SEXY BEE! She is always smiling, always pleasant, always professional, her briefcase in tow, and heading straight to the office where her new bosses are expecting her as she strides in. The men can't take their eyes off her and the women don't know what to expect of her, but if put to any test, she will eat there asses up. Shy is well schooled and well prepared with a mind like a steel strap within her. All young black women are well represented in this competitive business world. Shy spends the rest of the day wowing the bosses and locking up her position in the firm as the new hotshot lawyer.

At the end of the day, the big boss asked Shy to have a word in his office. He tells her about his wife and how they've been married forty-one years and how he's never seen any attraction in any other woman since the day he met her and how he never will. How he hopes everyone gets married to the love of their life like he did and for her to be sure to keep work and personal life separate, no client relationships at any cost. He stands up shakes her hand says, "Welcome to my firm Shy. Let's walk out together to close your first day. Tomorrow you'll start meeting clients. Oh, I almost forgot another young hotshot lawyer heading up our creative arts division." He opens the door that is joining his office, and he says, "I'd like you to meet my son Stacey."

THE END.

THE SADIE HAWKINS SURPRISE

By Brian Robinson Sr.

THE SADIE HAWKINS SURPRISE

Three women all 39 years old and who graduated from college together host a special event every three years for the alumni who aren't married. They call it **"The Sadie Hawkins Surprise"**. It's an entire weekend of female generated events that the women drive, and they control who's aggressively going to pursue whom from buying drinks, asking for a dance, dinner invites, and finally, the room key offering of which you have two hours to show up. The way this works is everyone attending has to RSVP five months in advance, so the women would already have an idea of who they would like to spend time pursuing. The men really don't have a choice of who is interested in them. They have to just go with the flow of things, and if they receive an offer not to their liking, they can just decline. The women who organize it aren't married, and are not in serious relationships, which is the general idea of how it's suppose to work; and if you have a commitment with another you don't RSVP.

Toni is sitting on her bed reading a cookbook recipe when her phone rings, it's her friend Dee. She gets excited and closes her book and answers, "What's up Freaky Dee?" "Everything Freaky Tee, can't wait to see you guys," she replied. "I just finished shopping again, and it's so many new things I want. I love when the weather breaks, what are you doing? Sitting home reading I bet!" Dee said. "Yeah you're right," Toni replies, "are we going to conference with the trouble maker or what? She said she would be waiting on our call." "In five minutes," Dee responds, "I know exactly what she is doing, and she needs more time." "Y'all so stank," Toni stated. "No, not that...she's trying to save the world again, one bad-ass kid at a time. You know she's always looking out for everyone before herself, but we gonna get her on some real selfish shit on our weekend, and it's coming up for us all. I've seen the RSVP list, and my first choice is at the top of the list, and I'm looking forward to tasting him," Dee replied.

After Toni and Dee share a laugh, they both received a text from the third of the three partners in crime, "Wink." She is the no nonsense, smart, laid back, and unofficial leader of the crew. The text reads, *"I kno u witches r talkin abt me, conference me n please."* Toni tells Dee to conference her in. Dee tells her to hold on and dials her in. The three share the usual greeting in harmony, "What's up hussyyyyy?" "We good with everything so far?" Wink asked. "Yeah Dee," Toni replied, "yeah we're good, your brothers coming in about five Sunday morning, do you need me to ride with you? Hopefully, I'll be too worn out from Saturday's extracurricular activities to be awake." "Yeah me too; I hope," Toni stated, "I don't have the greatest feeling that I'll get who and what I've been hoping for all this time, but we'll see." "If he doesn't show," Wink replied, "fuck him, it's his loss." "Look y'all, don't take all the fun out the weekend by limiting your options to spend time getting to know someone you never looked at that way before, that's what it's about, us getting to choose them and not them choosing us. Let's just keep that in mind and have a great time." "Ok," Dee stated, "so is J coming and if so, will you choose him?" "I might let him pick up my scent," Wink replied, "I haven't decided yet." "Yeah right," Dee said, "so if not him than who else Wink?" "I don't know?" Wink replied, "I heard your daddy was coming; that's my first choice." They all busted out laughing. "Seriously y'all," Toni stated, "I can't stop thinking of having a new experience doing something different with someone new." "Then do it," Wink replied, "just don't limit yourself and make sure you protect your heart and your body." "Yes call the Trojan mannnnn," he said. "B.Y.O.C., bring your own condoms!" Dee shouted.

The daily conversations and laughs continue with the ladies leading up to the big weekend events. Wink, Toni, and Dee all fly out on Wednesday morning, which allows them to have an evening to themselves before things start rolling, and before the former classmates start arriving. The ladies haven't seen each other face to face in a minute, and they all really miss and love one another, so it's a joyous reunion.

After they arrive and after all the hugs, love, and tears, they make their way to the hotel to get themselves checked in. Afterwards, they meet downstairs for dinner and drinks to discuss their free time for that evening, and for the next day. Wink takes the opportunity to remind the ladies not to invest time in people who may not have them on their radar, and to try to enjoy and explore new possibilities.

After dinner was over, Wink goes upstairs to change before they hit the town on their own. She's on the phone with Kevin, who's the object of Toni's desire. "Come on man, no bullshitting, just tell me if you're feeling her the way she's feeling you! If not it's kool, I'll just try to keep her focusing on other things, so she won't get too caught up. You know I don't wanna see my girls get hurt or disappointed," Wink stated, "I know you gotta keep your options open; I'm not trying to steer you wrong Kev, just let me in on that one thing, so I can have her head ready for that let down if it comes. You're my homie, and I got love for you! I won't tell anyone else, I promise, and if your other thing don't work out she'll be available, ok; I got it." Wink hangs up the phone and says to herself, "Bitch ass nigga!"

Wink sits for a minute and thinks about calling Chris, the guy that Dee really wants to see, but she changes her mind and fixes herself a drink, and decides not to. "My girls deserve better than this," she says to herself, "I just want to see them happy, is that too much to ask? God damn, pretty boys on some real punk shit." She makes her next call to Toni. "Let's go get into some real fun shit somewhere," she said, "let's go see some strippers right now!" "Guys, right?" Toni replied back. "Girls we might learn some new tricks," Wink stated, "I gotta pole in my basement!" "You're nasty," Toni replied. "Look witch, you know your momma had a pole in your bassinet and you still under achieved; now call Dee and be ready in thirty minutes, we got tricks to learn," Wink stated.

The minute the ladies arrived, they realized that they were in the right place to see both men and women in the same building, but on two different floors. As usual, Wink has it all planned out, and getting the ladies into some fun and trouble is her specialty. "Ok," Wink said out loud, "who we doin' first, ladies or men?" Dee was the first one to respond, "Let's watch the women first." "Girl, did you change up your diet without telling me?" Wink said. "Shut your mouth and let's go in," Dee, shot back.

Wink gets the first good spot available to sit. She opens her bag and pulls out a few items. Toni's jaw drops in amazement. "What the fuck," Toni said, "why do you have a rubber glove in your bag? Oh Shit, is that baby oil? "I knew it," Dee stated, "she's an ass rapper!" Wink laughed so hard she could barely speak. "I might wanna smack some asses on the men's floor, and I don't want no butt sweat on my hands," Wink replied laughing uncontrollably.

Dee is really paying special attention to this one girl,

and real close attention to her dance moves. She wants to learn how to dance that way. She signed up for a pole dancing class before, but never went. She's been feeling very adventurist lately, especially leading up to this weekend. How can she not, but something extra is brewing up inside her that her lucky choice may get a hold of this weekend.

Wink is drawing a bit of attention from some of the female dancers and shoots off a look to say, "Backup; I'm just here to watch and learn at the same time." She notices that Dee is getting more and more connected with this one girl, and remembers when Dee dated a woman once for a short time while they were in school. She decides to give Dee some space because Toni doesn't know about Dee's interest in women. Wink leans over to Dee and says, "Look; we're gonna go check out the men's lineup, and we will be back to check on you." "Take your time ok," Dee said. "OoooKay, watch what you eat girl," Wink said jokingly. "Oh girl go, I'll meet you up there," said Dee, "you taking Toni with you right, cause she not ready for this yet." "Exactly," Wink replied.

Dee waits until the coast is clear and summons over the waitress for two apple martinis, and then summons over the female dancer that she's been watching for a lap dance. Two guys sitting next to Dee are looking on as she turns to them and says, "Oh yeah playya, you got company in here tonight; in fact, if you pay for our drinks, I might get her number for you and give you mine too!" Dee laughs aloud.

Wink and Toni walk in upstairs, and Wink spots a male dancer she'd seen before. "Oh I liked his show in D.C.," Wink said, "I was meaning to smack that ass there, but I wasn't close enough." Wink starts putting on her rubber glove. "Come here boy let me smack that ass. I should've bought some plastic wrap, so I can get a lap dance. Fuck it, I'm getting a lap dance, and witch you're getting one too," Wink insisted. "What if I don't want a lap dance Wink?" Toni stated. "I will pull one of them tracks out your head. Come on, stop thinking about that nigga and have some fun girl. If he comes...he comes, if he don't, fuck him," said Wink. She wasted no time in speaking her mind and said, "Oh shit, look at the thighs on that boy, tell me you don't wanna squeeze that butt? Come on Toni! Hey! Hey! Can I get a drink over here? They should've told y'all I was coming because I'm here!"

The strip club was more fun than Dee expected it to be and a bit too much for poor Toni, but they still had a blast; how can you not hanging with Wink? "What did you do all night Dee?" Toni asked, "you smell like a drunk." "Your mother smells like a drunk," Dee replied. Toni and Dee cried with laughter. They continued to poke fun at a very tipsy Dee as they set out to find food for their empty stomachs and coffee before they continue on with their night.

The ladies stopped at a popular all night breakfast spot. While sitting at the table, Wink notices some of the alumni that are in town for the Sadie Hawkins Surprise that are in the diner to have a late-night meal as well. Wink Jumps up with excitement and quickly walks over to their table. Sitting there is her friend Minnie aka Tiny, she is the head of a group of women who call themselves "The Big Girls Club", their model is, "They do big girl shit!" Wink and Tiny both exchange a big hug when Tiny Jumps right into the weekend and its events. "Now you know we ain't bullshitting with no chump shit," Tiny stated, "I got all the things I need, and I got my sights set on that pretty-boy basketball star, and I dare him not to show. I'm gonna get mine this time; he owes me!" Tiny and Wink share a giggle. "You are sick girl," Wink stated, "what if he don't show, what you gonna do with your crazy self then?" "Who you calling crazy? I heard you were at the strip club smacking every ass in the joint with your rubber glove on," Tiny replied. They laughed again. "Sure was," Wink said, "I would've smacked your big ass if you were there too." The girls could not stop laughing. "Look," Tiny insisted, "seriously I think we gonna kidnap Stan for a few hours, don't say nothing." Wink now realizing she is serious blurts out, "Oh my fucking god!" "Wink that nigga owes me! He played me, and I did all that work with him, so he could catch up on his work and still play ball, and all I wanted was to slam his tall skinny ass down on my bunk one good time!" said Tiny. "Ok Tiny, do you playya, but you know me, I ain't checking for no bitch ass nigga. If I'm feeling you and you miss me...you miss out! Fuck old times make new times you know!" Wink replied.

"Tiny, umm, I love all my girls, and I hope everyone enjoy themselves and make some memories; that's why we came here," Wink implied, while staring with a devilish grin. "Why every time I see you, you look like you up to something?" Tiny stated. "Cause I'm always up to something," Wink replied, "look I'll see you at the cookout tomorrow." Wink goes back to the table with her friends, and they finish off the night.

A day later at the cookout most of the people expected is in attendance and things are really beginning to take shape. There is much socializing going on as well as a pre-party feeling out going on too with plenty of lust in the air, but Wink seems to be preoccupied and Dee notices it and approaches her. "What's up with you mama?" Dee asked, "you're not your usual self Wink." "Well, I'm worried about Toni. I think Kev is gonna play her wrong," Wink stated, "I'm also worried about picking up my brother Sunday morning. It's not good timing on his part, but I'm trying to make it work. I don't wanna tell my dad to drive all the way here to pick him up since he's not well just because I might be doing it or something the night before. No matter how old you get, you never want to tell your daddy you're doing it...you know!" Dee and Wink enjoy a few moments of laughter.

Wink decides to take matters into her own hands and decides to press the issue with Kev to see if he intends to pick Toni or not. She first recalls in her mind the time Kev came to her dorm room when they were freshmen's and how he tried to kiss her before he started dating Toni. She wonders if Kev wanting her could be the reason he won't pick Toni, and she's hoping not. Wink calls Kev, "What's up Wink?" "Don't what's up me nigga, why you play'n? I'm just trying to look out for my girl, and she was really looking forward to seeing you," Wink sarcastically replied. "She will see me and I'll see her," Kev replied, "why are you trying to make up my mind for me? I thought this was about the women choosing and the men responding! You're a control freak Wink!" "Nigga you know what? You just pushed the bitch button. Now you enjoy yourself the best way you can, cause I'm gonna make sure the best-looking women in the place think you're a fucking fag!" "Ok, ok, ok," Kev said, "I'll choose your girl Wink." "No the fuck you won't," Wink drastically stated, "my friend is no charity case; she just happens to really like your sorry ass, and it might be time she just gets over it and move on." "I said I'll choose her Wink, god damn!" Kev said. "No, no just stay away because it will only make things worse. She needs to switch her focus anyway and have some fun, so fuck you! You come near her and I'll mace you, bust your fuck'n head wide open, and leave you with your pants pulled down around your ankles. You know I'm not fuck'n around; CLICK!!!" she yelled. She slams her phone shut and whispers to herself, "Bitch ass nigga!"

Wink places her next call to Chris. "What's up man? I know this is a little bit out of order for the way things are supposed to go, and I know you're gonna have your plate pretty full, but is Dee anywhere on your radar because you know she always puts her all into her friendship with men, and it always seems to fall apart when things look promising," said Wink. Chris said, "Look Wink, let me stop you. I wish I had a friend like you. I really like Dee, but Wink, I know a lot about women, and I don't believe you can help her with what she really seeks. I think I know what her fantasy is, and she will never tell you. It just has to happen all at once and just fall into place." "Did she ever tell you?" Wink inquisitively asked. "No Wink, but I got a pretty good idea of what her twist is, so just fall back ma! I will share one thought; she may not always prefer just one!" said Chris. Wink was puzzled. "Oookay," she mumbled. Chris continued, "This is going to be a fun weekend, and if you don't enjoy yourself... you're not trying to. Wink, I know they don't have the same appeal as they use to and neither of them are as hot as you. You've managed to keep your good looks in perfect condition, and you're still half crazy, but if they find out what you're up to it may hurt them more than any guy could. So if you need me to do something just tell me." "No I'll just fall back, but thanks Chris, I needed that, and if you get someone you really like and really want, go enjoy yourself and remember it's not just about sex ok?" Wink said. "Ok Wink thanks, and see you later ma," said Chris. "Hey Chris," Wink quickly blurted out, "If you don't get none you gotta be gay." Wink cries with laughter with Chris following behind her. "Come on wit da bullshit Wink!" said Chris. "Cause man," Wink stated, "you always say the right shit. You like Dr. Ruth with black balls." Wink and Chris share a few more laughs before they hang up.

Wink gets busy making more plans for picking up her brother and organizing the women for the party night. She is heard telling groups of women that they need to wear tight black dresses, high heels, pushup bras, and the smallest panties they can find to the dance.

Finally, it's the Sadie Hawkins Dance night. There is nowhere to run to and nowhere to hide once you're inside. It's like Vegas! Everyone has been enjoying themselves, and got dolled up for this special night. There is not a bad hairdo in the house. The ladies are all well put together this evening, as are the men. Beards trimmed, cologne just right, shoes and games are tight; the men are cocky, confident, and ready to be chosen.

Wink is responsible for putting all of this together, so she remains the unofficial host of these events, which will require her to say a few words of welcoming and thanking all her single ladies for coming and making this all possible. She also reminds them that it's about having fun and socializing, not just about having sex. Wink ends her speech with her slogan, "It's much more fun if you can get you some, enjoy y'all."

Wink spots Kev over by the bar eyeing things out, and decides to make peace with him; but at the same time feeling like she shouldn't have got that deep. "Hey man," she said as she approached him, "I just want to say it's not that deep, and I apologize, we kool?" "My feelings are still hurt. I thought we was better than that Wink?" Kev replied. "We are; that's why I'm standing here without my mace. I'll buy you a drink," said Wink. "It's open bar girl! You really wanna make it up to me?" Kev asked her. "I'm listening Kev," said Wink. "Give me your room key," he said, "there are no limits and no restrictions right? Everybody here is grown, and it would be just between us Wink." "You're not supposed to ask for a key it's supposed to be offered," said Wink. "So offer if you wanna make it up to me Wink," said Kev. "If I did that I'd have to switch rooms first," replied Wink. "I'll be here til it's over Wink," he says while wearing a devilish grin. Wink touches his hand and turns away.

Wink is thinking to herself, *now I know why he never went after Toni.* All this time he's been plotting on me. Still, I should have told her what I really thought way back in school. I hope she's not in love with this fool; I hope it's just that he's sexy. Fuck all that, he needs to be taken down a few notches. Tonight I'll keep telling these fuckers, "You fuck wit the terrorists you get blown up!"

About an hour later, Wink goes back to Kev after making about ten phones calls in the lobby. "Look man," she said, "If we do this you have to go ahead of me before anyone notices you're gone. I won't leave till it's over that way I can avoid any questions. Ok, deal." "Deal," said Kev, "I'll leave now, take a shower and wait for you ok Wink?" Kev said. "Kool Kev," replied Wink. "You won't be sorry in the morning," Kev stated, "I promise that." And strolls off. Wink picks up her phone and barely talking out loud, "It's on, he coming now." Toni approaches and Wink quickly hang up. "Have you seen Kev?" Toni asked Wink, "he seems like he was avoiding me." "He is, I told you I think he's gay. His ass is starting to poke out too much Toni," replied Wink. "I think I just wanna get as drunk as I can stand tonight, then I'll really have some fun Wink," said Toni. "Don't get hit with rape charges playya, just grown men now you hear," Wink said jokingly.

In the room upstairs that Wink just rented, Kev is getting in the shower. His clothes are all over the bathroom as if he couldn't wait to get out of them. He hops in the bathroom and gets in the nice and steamy shower for about fifteen minutes, but when he gets out, he notices that there is a note on the sink that wasn't there before he got in the shower. He also notices that "Freddie Jackson's" music is playing in the other room; the note and the music draws a fist pump from him. The note reads, "I've been thinking of this for about 20yrs. I need you to take your time. I need you to hold me first for just a few minutes, so I can get past my nervousness. I want to feel your arms around me really tight for a few minutes, and then you may do to me whatever you please. Put your condoms on before you get in the bed if it's now."

Kev is more than ready and excited and out of his mind. To him, Wink is his forbidden fruit, the one he could never get to. He's not in-love with her; he just needs to conquer and control her, to break down her strong will and try to punish her. Kev lotions up his body, rolls on his protection and while still grooving to the music, he slowly pulls open the door to the candle-lit room with rose peddles on the floor. He walks across the rose peddles that lead to the bed and thinks to himself, "How in to me has she always been? I'm gonna tear that ass up and shut down that smartass mouth." He takes a swallow of the wine that's been poured for him, drops his towel and slides under the covers and raps his arms around? What appears to be a warm, firm, but strong body and grabs hold of very unpleasant hairy balls. Surprise, as he jumps up screaming, "What the fuck man! What the fuck man! What the Fucking Fuck!!!" It's not Wink of course; it's a guy name Charles, a friend of Winks from the strip club. Charles is a gay dancer, wearing nothing but his blonde braids as he jumps up butt naked. Almost instantly, Wink and Chris pops out of the closet. "Surprise Nigga!" Wink and Chris shouted in unity, while snapping the picture of the two naked men just about to face off. "April Fool, fool!" Wink yelled out. "Man this is fucked-up Wink!" Kev yelled. "No, fucked up would be if this picture got on Facebook, or the video from Chris's phone made it to YouTube; and why is your dick still hard? Not a good look that's a naked boy," replied Wink. Her and Chris still laughing as they exit the room.

Kev now trying to put his pants on. "Chris, yo Chris hold up cuz, don't do me like that man. Wink I was just fucking with you to see if you would really go through with it, hold up y'all," he pleaded as they walked into the elevator laughing out of control as the doors closed.

Meanwhile, Dee is in her room, and she decided not to give Chris her Key after all. Instead, she offered it to a mystery person she had been attracted to from afar and is not expecting that they will show up. It was kind of a long shot in her mind until she got a knock at the door. She jumped up and ran over to look through the peephole, at the same time turning to cover her mouth while whispering, "What the fuck!" Dee takes a deep breath then opens the door, and there stands a very attractive married couple, Troy and Lisa who are both dentists, that she befriended the last time she stayed in the area. They met at a friend's pool party who told her the couple desires three-way sex and with Dee feeling very adventurist at the time gave Lisa a call. She invites them in. The room has a very cozy intimate setting, dimly lit candles, wine and champagne and soft music. Dee has to do some feeling out while she is very attracted to Lisa. Troy, on the other hand, is a bit of a jackass sometimes.

The three sit and chat for a minute over wine just to catch up a bit. Dee and Lisa are truly feeling one another. Troy is feeling a bit left out early in the game and decides to make his presence felt by opening his mouth at a few untimely moments before excusing himself to the rest room. While he is away, the women have a minute to assess that Dee is really not feeling Troy, so it wouldn't work out.

Meanwhile, Troy in all his arrogance is in the bathroom with his shirt off getting his manhood worked up for the kill. (Note to the Brothers - "If you find yourself in this kind of situation..." SHUT WHAT WE CALL THE HELL UP! and let the ladies use you, however they may; you won't be sorry. Well, that's what I heard anyway!) Troy busts out of the bathroom with his shirt off and his gun in hand. "Come on fool," Lisa said to Troy, "Dee is having unexpected company, and you're always jumping the gun with your gun!" Troy, while very good-looking and classroom smart, has no swagger or street smarts. It sometimes takes away from the game they are to play. He immediately shows his no swagger. "Damn, I thought we were staying," Troy said, "she's too old anyway, let's bounce."

Dee is alone once her guest leaves, but she gets a call from Toni with Wink on the line too. "Hey I guess everyone is still up and alone past the deadline huh?" Wink stated, "well listen, I got an issue. My dad had car trouble, and my brother came in early, but caught a cab here. I'm on my way to pick up my dad, so could you guys go down and get my brother and put him in one of your rooms and bunk together till I get back." "Yeah," Dee said, "no problem girl, is he downstairs? Does he have his uniform on cause we don't know what he looks like?" "Yes," Wink replied, "he's in uniform. He's tall, thin, and has a handsome twenty-two-year-old face; you can't miss him." "Ok," said Toni, "we'll get him settled; no worries just take care of your dad." "Oh, do you need me to go with you Wink?" Dee asked. "No, I got Charles with me Dee," said Toni. "Who, Wink?" she asked. "I'll tell you about it later, thanks girls I'm hanging up," said Toni.

Dee and Toni met at the elevator, and both go down to meet Ty. Ty is a tall thin-built young man and strikingly handsome. They approach, introduce, and exchange hugs when Ty lets them know he's in need of a drink and invites them to sit a while. They have a drink and decide that he can finish off the wine and champagne bottles left untouched in one of the rooms since they have plenty.

While walking back to Dee's room Ty mentions that he has something to talk to Wink about. Dee informs him that Wink won't be back until morning, and asks him if everything is ok. "Yes and no, can I talk to you guys about it?" Ty asked, "I'm kind of embarrassed, but I need some quick help." "Sure," Toni replied, "whatever we can do; what's up Ty?" "I met this girl on the ship that I was stationed on, and we formed a bond. It was really, really strong, and I need to be with her, but it's not allowed on the ship. It was a special exercise, so nothing special happened between us. I mean, she's been in a long relationship before, and she's a few years older than me, but I barley know how to hold a woman. When I'm dancing I think I love her, and my friends are telling me I should go get some high-price hookers to tune up. I'm not feeling that shit, and my dad and I just don't talk about stuff like that. He's been married to the same woman all his life. He don't know nothing!" Ty said.

The three arrived to Dee's room, and Ty continues, "Besides, I don't want him telling me how he boned my mom you know!" Ty, Dee, and Toni cracked up laughing. "Come here boy," Dee said, "have another drink, and Toni is gonna show you how to hold her when you dance, and I'll give you a few pointers on what not to say and how to just be you." "I want to put all of me inside of her heart and soul," Ty stated, "I know this is weird, but I need to know how to be a perfect kisser, will y'all please, please help me out?"

After a short glance at each other, Toni stated, "I'm gonna need more wine Dee; open another bottle." The three finished off a third bottle of wine and one bottle of champagne. "Ok soldier boy," Dee stated, "take that jacket off and let's see if you can dance." "I'm a little drunk I think," Ty replied while taking off his jacket as Dee requested. Then his uniform shirt, and showing off his wifebeater with the U.S Navy stitching. Ty, while thinly built is very manly and has muscles all over in perfect shape. Toni takes a double look at his attractive body after he discarded his uniform shirt and glasses, and notices that he's quite the looker. She's warm and tipsy, but takes hold of him as if Dee is not even in the room. She starts dancing very close, and asks him to hold her tighter as they grind to the music. Dee, still sitting on the bed; she turns the bottle up and takes a big gulp. "Should I do what comes natural now like you said?" Ty asked Toni. With her face pressed against his chest, she whispers, "Yessss!" Ty puts his left hand on the small of her back and lightly runs his fingers down to her waist and slides them down the side of her hip to her thigh, then softly grips her right butt cheek with his left hand and pulls her tighter, then whispers, "Is that ok?" Toni now consumed in the moment sighs, "Yessss!" Ty wets his lips before sliding them cross Toni's ear then onto her neck as her body reaches a near boiling point. She feels a slight trickle, and has lost all that better judgment that would've normally stopped her about two bottles ago.

Little Ty looks up, and locks eyes with Dee, whose unmet urges have gotten her nipples bricked right then and there. Ty raising his two fingers at Dee summons her to join in the erotic moment. Dee's body now oozing with all kinds of desires falls deep under the spell of the moment. As it appears, little Ty has turned tiger like "Tiger Woods", maybe not as inexperienced as he led on. As Dee joins the dance, he raps his long arms partly around her pressing her against Toni. Toni gets goose bumps from Dee's warmth, thinking to herself, *I don't know what's going down, but it's going down. I'm just so wide open, the hell with it,* as she offers her lips to Ty's for a first kiss. Ty receives her lips, and quickly spins her around so that Dee is at his back. He reaches his hand around her to grip her ass, pulling her to press against him. She licks his neck while rubbing his shoulders gently, she whispers, "Let's have it." Dee wildly pulls Ty's shirt over his head and tosses it. Toni still a little overwhelmed does know whose lead to follow as she quickly goes from teacher to student. Ty and Dee being the aggressors, and Dee understanding the entire situation backs off just a tad while Ty seduces the rest of Toni's clothes off. All of Dee's delight she aides him in his seduction.

He picks up Toni allowing her to wrap her legs around his shoulders as he walks her to the bed, lays her on her back, and takes a soft lipped bite of her warm juiciness and pleasuring her into an instant erotic explosion, slowly letting up. Dee, not to be left out, slides her body between the bed and his crouch and begins to pleasure him the same, and thinking only to herself, "Yeah, this shit is off the hook in here."

Ty's in some kind of a groove changing one condom after the other, satisfying both women one after the other, sometimes at the same time, giving both women a night filled with first after first. It's more than filling as Toni is the first to get over excited from multiples and too much wine, passing out while Ty continues to sweat Dee's hair into an afro over another hour of erotic explosions.

Suddenly, the loud ringing phone wakes Toni, and it's now morning. Dee is stretched across the blanket on the floor, and the shower is running. "Oh fuck that's Wink on the phone," Toni stated nervously, "what the hell did we do?" She tries to jump up, but last nights' wine pulls her ass right back down. She grabs her head and stands up slowly then grabs her butt. She knocks on the bathroom door and pushes it open, only to see the sink running, but Ty is gone. Toni wakes Dee and says, "What the fuck, where is he? He's not here Dee." "Shit we gotta find him Toni," said Dee. "Before he tells Wink," Toni replied. "Damn Toni, we both need to marry that nigga before he screws that ship trick, he was a monster. We gonna have to change our religion," said Dee. "This shit ain't funny Dee. We fucked our best friend's lil brother and damn near each other," said Toni. "Yeah," Dee replied, "no I think we fucked each other." "Oh my god what have we done," Toni frantically stated. "I don't know what you did Toni, but I got mine, and I needed too. Now we can put this away and never talk about it again. That's the normal script for this weekend anyway, so calm your ass down and stick to it," said Dee. "I don't know if I can Dee," replied Toni. "Whatever, do what you gotta do!" said Dee.

The phone rings again, and it's still Wink. Dee finally answers, "Witches will y'all get down here and say hi to my dad and bye to me. I'm outta here, and I ordered y'all breakfast on me," said Wink. "Ok we're coming now, did you see Ty?" Dee asked. "Sure did," Wink replied, "come on we gotta go." They hung up, got themselves together, and went downstairs. Wink is sitting at the table alone with an angelic grin on her face. "Y'all looked whipped on like two beat up witches," Wink Stated, "wave to my dad in the black truck, he's riding back with a friend of mines from back home." "Look Wink," Toni said hesitantly, "I gotta tell you something, and it's crazy. You my girl and I can't keep this shit." "Not now, in two minutes drippy mouth," cutting Toni off, "I need you to meet someone very special to me." "Who is that?" Toni asked. A tall, well-built, clean, cute, brown-skinned man approached, and Wink said, "I like you meet my little brother Ty."

Both women are stunned and just stared at him. "Hello ladies..." IT'S NOT THE MAN THEY HOSTED ALL NIGHT. "Y'all ok?" Wink asked. "Who the hell was that we picked up from here last night?" Dee asked. "I knew them sorry ass niggers you two messed with wasn't gonna get it done, so I had a backup plan for my girls. He practices the safest sex, and never quits early, so I'm told. Call me, gotta go," said Wink as she bounces out the door. Not before turning and pointing to a note, she left on the table. Dee grabs the note and tares it open; it's an invite to a secret all woman's social group called 'GT' stands for "-------" THE END.

ABOUT THE AUTHOR

Brian Robinson Sr. was born and raised in Philadelphia, PA in North Philly (Nicetown) section of the city. He is the seventh of eight children of Emory and Helen Howell.

He attended Simon Gratz High School and Delaware Valley College briefly, before leaving early for personal reasons, and entering into a street life, which shaped him into a man with many stories to tell, and cautions for the youth to help provide better decision making.

Brian is a very creative man with an edge for short stories without cutting the Meat and Juice.

Stay tuned for many more books, The Gifted Child, Yes I Am, Gritty City 215 to name a few, and potential film projects.

If you would like to contact Brian directly, reach out to him on:

Email: BiiwiiR@gmail.com

Facebook: https://www.facebook.com/brianiiwii.robinson

Twitter: @BiiwiiR

9 780989 265652